SPHDZ

Book #1!

Space

SPHDZ

Book #1!

headz

by Jon Scieszka

Made extra-strength by
Francesco Sedita

Illustrated by
Shane Prigmore

Simon & Schuster Books for Young Readers
New York London Toronto Sydney SPHDZ

SIMON
BOOKS FOR YOUNG READERS
An imprint of Simon & Schuster Children's Publishing Di...
1230 ... of the Americas
New York, New ... 10020

Text copyright © 2010 by JRS Wo...
... copyright © 2010 by Shane Prigmore
... reserved, including the ...
... whole or in pa...

... Simon & Schu... ... information
... about special discount... purchase...
... tact Simon & Schu... Special Sales ... 8...
... 50... ...9 or busi...@simon...uster.co... the
Simon & Schuster ... Speakers B... ...th...
live event. For more information... ...er... ant...
Simon & Schuster ... Speakers Bureau ... 1-866-2...
... ...our website at ...mon...rs.co... ...an
... • The text ...is b... ...n Joppa... ...strations for
... rendered ... ...anufactured in the United States
of ... ...41...
... 6 8 ... ... 7 5 3 1

...rary of Congress Catalog...
Data • Sci...a, ...book...
#1 ...son ... ...and Fran...
cesco ... edit... ...ter...
Shane Prigmore, ill. ... cm
... (Spaceheadz ; #1) ...
... ...t at Brooklyn's P.S. 83...
... ...ed ... is ...
... ...nge studen...
...ly ...s to b... ... ...gia...
... ...t his ... ...e has trouble ...
anyone else o... ... ... ISBN ...
4169-7951-... ...ard... ...er...
[1. Extraterrestri... be... ...ti... ...n...Fiction.
3. Spies—Fiction ... Moving ... ...n. 5. Family
...York (State)—New York—Fict... ...rooklyn (New York, N.Y.)—Fiction.]
...Francesco. II. Prigmore, Shane, ill. III. Title. • PZ7.S41267So 2010 • [Fic]—
...2010001983 • ISBN 978-1-4169-8705-5 (eBook)

first edition

To the _____ and _____ _____ional SPHDZ of PS _____ _____m, Addy, Andrea,
Bianca, B_____ Carlyle, Cedrick, David, _____ J_____ _____an, Jose, Kristin
Lily, Mickel, Nelson, Peyt_____ _____ _____ _____teven.
To their very SPHDZ te_____ _____ _____mil____
And to their ultimate SPH_____ princip_____ _____
—J. S.

To Kent and Marian Prigmo_____ _____nk _____r _____g _____ur s_____ _____r _____ u____
b_____ _____HDZ _____u guy____
_____P.

SIMON + SCHUSTER
BOOKS FOR YOUNG READERS
An imprint of Simon + Schuster
Children's Publishing Division
1230 Avenue of the Americas,
New York, New York 10020

SIMON + SCHUSTER BOOKS FOR YOUNG READERS is a trademark of Simon + Schuster, Inc. • For information about special discounts for bulk purchases, please contact Simon + Schuster Special Sales at 1-866-506-1949 or business@simonandschuster.com. • The Simon + Schuster Speakers Bureau can bring authors to your live event. For more information or to book an event, contact the Simon + Schuster Speakers Bureau at 1-866-248-3049 or visit our website at www.simonspeakers.com. • Book design by Dan Potash • The text for this book is set in Joppa. • The illustrations for this book are rendered digitally. • Manufactured in the United States of America, 0410 FFG
2 4 6 8 10 9 7 5 3 1
Library of Congress Cataloging-in-Publication Data • Scieszka, Jon. • SPHDZ book #1! / Jon Scieszka with Francesco Sedita ; illustrated by Shane Prigmore. — 1st ed. • p. cm. — (Spaceheadz ; #1) • Summary: On his first day at Brooklyn's P.S. 858, fifth-grader Michael K. is teamed with two very strange students, and while he gradually comes to believe they are aliens who need his help, he has trouble convincing anyone else of the truth. • ISBN 978-1-4169-7951-7 (hardcover : alk. paper) [1. Extraterrestrial beings—Fiction. 2. Schools—Fiction. 3. Spies—Fiction. 4. Moving, Household—Fiction. 5. Family life—New York (State)—New York—Fiction. 6. Brooklyn (New York, N.Y.)—Fiction.] I. Sedita, Francesco. II. Prigmore, Shane, ill. III. Title. IV. Title: SPHDZ book number one! • PZ7.S41267So 2010 • [Fic]—dc22 • 2010001983 • ISBN 978-1-4169-8705-5 (eBook)

first edition

To the original and inspirational SPHDZ of P.S. 58: Adam, Addy, Andrea, Bianca, Brad, Carlyle, Cedrick, David, Evie, Jonathan, Jordan, Jose, Kristin, Lily, Mickel, Nelson, Peyton, Reginn, Ryan, and Steven.

To their very SPHDZ teachers Sandi and Emily.

And to their ultimate SPHDZ principal, Giselle.

—J. S.

To Kent and Marian Prigmore. Thanks for letting your son grow up to be a SPHDZ. I love you guys.

—S. P.

SPACEHEADZ ATTACK!

βπåς´´´ådΩ åttåς°∕

Michael K. knew his first day in a new school in a new city was going to be weird. How could a first day at someplace in Brooklyn, New York, called P.S. 858 not be weird?

He just had no idea it could be this weird.

Michael K. had been in fifth grade for only twenty minutes, and already

1. Mrs. Halley had stuck him in the slow group with the two strange new kids,

2. the new girl had eaten half of his only pencil, and

3. the new boy had just told Michael K. that they were Spaceheadz from another planet.

1

"Uh, yeah," said Michael K. "I just moved here too."

The girl flexed an arm. "**SMACKDOWN**," she said in a voice like a wrestling announcer.

"Very nice." Michael K. nodded.

Sure, he was a new kid too. But these other new kids were seriously creeping him out. He did not want to get stuck with these losers on the first day of school. It could ruin his whole life.

The boy nodded back. "*JUST DO IT*."

The girl drew on her *Star Wars* lunch box:

This was getting beyond weird.

"Michael K., *I'M LOVING IT!*" said the boy. "We need your help. You must become a SPHDZ. Save your world. I am Bob."

"Jennifer," said the girl in that deep, echoing voice.

Michael K. watched Jennifer crunch the last of his Dixon Ticonderoga No. 2.

How did this new kid Bob know his name? Michael K. hadn't said it. What did he mean, "save your world"? Were they just messing with him? Yeah, that was it. They were just goofing around.

Michael K. decided he would goof right back . . . then move his seat as far away from them as possible.

"I get it," said Michael K. "You are Spaceheadz from another planet. On a mission to Earth. Here to take over the world. Take me to your leader. Bzzt, bzzzt."

"See! I told you, Jennifer!" said Bob. "Michael K. can do anything! He is like a rock. **_MMM, MMM GOOD_**."

Jennifer burped up the eraser from Michael K.'s only pencil. She spit it out.

"SPHDZ—**_GET RRRREADY TO RRRRRUMBLE_**," said Jennifer.

"Eeek eek," said the class hamster.

Room 501-B went silent except for the sound of Mrs. Halley writing on the chalkboard.

The thought occurred to Michael K. that Bob and Jennifer were not joking.

The thought occurred to Michael K. that they really were Spaceheadz from another planet.

The thought exploded in Michael K.'s head that those thoughts were ridiculous.

Aliens don't invade fifth-grade classrooms. They don't look like fifth graders. And they don't talk like commercials and pro wrestlers.

Bob and Jennifer were probably just from somewhere else. And kind of confused.

Right.

Right?

Chapter 2

AGENT UMBER
å©´~† ¨µ∫´®

If it had been nighttime, a broken neon sign would have been buzzing and blinking a watery red light across the tiny, one-room apartment.

But it wasn't night-time. It was 9:42 in the morning. So a weak ray of sunlight and a lot of dust and zooming noises filled the small room.

The sunlight came from the sun, ninety-three million miles away. The dust and the noise came from the elevated Brooklyn-Queens Expressway, twenty-three feet away.

Agent Umber sat at his kitchen table. He ignored the dust and the zooming noises. He polished his already-shiny black shoes. He polished his already-shiny Anti-Alien Agency, or AAA for short, badge.

There were a million different stories in this town. You always had to be ready.

A ringing phone interrupted his polishing.

Umber picked up his AAA Picklephone® and listened.

"One, two," said a high-pitched voice on the other end.

Umber answered carefully, "Buckle my shoe."

"Alert level red," said the squeaky voice. "Alert level red. Possible AEW in your sector. We have detected waves from coordinates D-7. D-7. Proceed with extreme caution."

"Three, four," said Agent Umber. "I will shut the door."

This was *it*. A possible Alien Energy Wave. It was his chance to finally catch a real alien. It was his chance to get promoted and finally get a cool color name. A name like Agent Black or Agent Gray or even Agent Atomic Tangerine . . .

"And Umber?"

"Yes?"

"Do not make this another Fried Santa Incident. We do not want the publicity."

"Not a problem, Chief. That file has been buried for years."

"Then why am I reading about it right now on the 'Buzz' blog?"

Agent Umber looked at his Picklephone®. "I'm on it, Chief. I will not let the world down. I promise, as always, to Protect and to Serve and to Always Look Up."

The Picklephone® buzzed. Somewhere in the middle of that great speech it had lost service. Again. What a stupid idea for a phone. A pickle. That's what happens when you are the very last agent to pick a name and a phone. All of the cool phones are gone too.

But now all of that was going to change. Wow—a possible AEW. This was what every AAA agent lived for, hoped for, and polished his shoes for.

But first, thought Umber, I better just check the "Buzz" blog. Umber logged on to www.antialienagency .com. He clicked on "Agent Buzz." He froze.

"Oh, no." Umber covered his eyes. He couldn't take any more. It was all there—the whole embarrassing story for anyone who logged on to the site to read.

This was supposed to have been scrubbed at Top Level! Why was Agent Hot Magenta blabbing details all over the place?

Umber flipped his AAA Cereal Box Laptop® closed.

Well, he would show Hot Magenta. He would show the chief. He would show the world.

Agent Umber drew the black-out curtain across his one window.

He flipped open his AAA Coordinate Decoder®. He moved his aircraft carrier to one side and placed a single red peg in the hole at D-7.

He flipped off the overhead light and shined the light from his AAA Illuminator® to throw the image from the decoder onto his AAA Locator Grid®.

Agent Umber traced one finger across the line of D. He traced the other finger down the line of 7.

The rumble of one very large Coca-Cola delivery truck on the BQE shook the whole room.

Agent Umber's two fingers met at a small red square on the Brooklyn map.

ROOM 501-B
®ØØµ ∞º¡-∫

P.S. 858, room 501-B," said Mrs. Halley as she wrote the same on the upper right corner of the blackboard. "Your new home for this year. I like to say you are all Mrs. Halley's comets—out of this world!"

Bob and Jennifer jumped up and started hooting and cheering like a Nickelodeon awards-show audience.

The class hamster did three flips, then conked his head on the side of his food bowl.

"Oh my," said Mrs. Halley.

Mrs. Halley had been teaching at P.S. 858 for thirty-seven years. Thirty-six of those years she had taught fifth grade. But she had never seen anything quite like this.

"Thank you for your excitement," said Mrs. Halley. She adjusted her tiny glasses to scan her class list. She couldn't seem to find the names of these new students anywhere. Maybe that other new student in their group knew them.

"Michael K.? Could you explain to your friends that in this country we show our enthusiasm by remaining seated and clapping our hands."

"What? Huh? Me?" said Michael K. "Oh, no, I'm not Bob and Jennifer's friend. I don't even know them."

"Thank you, Michael K. Very helpful of you to tell me your friends' names." Mrs. Halley wrote "Bob" and "Jennifer" on the class list in her perfect handwriting. "And do you mind if I call you Michael K.? We have several Michaels this year, and your last name is such a long one. You may speak to your friends in your own language if you wish."

Bob and Jennifer hooted some more. Now

everyone in class was staring at Michael K. He had to do something.

"Sure, that's fine. But see, I don't really know— Bob and Jennifer, be quiet! Sit down!" said Michael K.

Bob and Jennifer sat down on the floor.

"No! Sit in your seats!"

Bob and Jennifer sat in their seats.

Mrs. Halley continued her beginning-of-the-year introduction like nothing had happened.

"And this year room 501-B will be on the World Wide Internet. Our new computer teacher, Mr. Boolean, helped me build our class website."

The girl behind Jennifer smiled at Michael K.

The kid next to her stopped drawing his comic to stare.

Mrs. Halley kept talking, more to herself than to the class. "Here we type in w-w-w-dot-m-r-s-h-a-l-l-e-y-s-c-o-m-e-t-s-dot-c-o-m. And there it is.

"Our class schedule. Your list of supplies. Class calendar. Assignments. And look—we can even see the weather. And lunch."

Bob made a face, showing his teeth to Michael K. "I am making a smile," he whispered. "I am happy Mission **SPHDZ** has begun. ***THINK OUTSIDE THE BUN***."

"Be **SPHDZ**," added Jennifer.

"Eeek eee eee we weeee," went the hamster.

"Yes, he can," Bob answered the hamster. "Michael K. can do anything."

Michael K. was afraid to ask, but he knew he had to. "And what's with the hamster?" He tried to keep his voice down, but the other kids were starting to look over.

"Major Fluffy?" said Bob. "Oh, he is the mission leader."

The hamster smiled at Michael K.

"**WE TRY HARDER**," said Bob. "SPHDZ want you."

The big kid in the back of the class twirled his finger around next to his big head in the universal signal for "Cuckoo!"

This was bad. Very bad.

"Don't talk to me," said Michael K.

WHY?

Σ˙Ϋ¿

The rest of the morning was just as strange as the beginning.

"Why?" Mrs. Halley repeated. "Why?"

In thirty-seven years of teaching, no child had ever asked why. These new Bulgarian or whatever-they-were students were really something.

"Well . . . it's just . . . just because that is what we do."

This did not answer Jennifer's question. At all.

This annoyed Jennifer.

The class lights dimmed. The clock behind Mrs. Halley spun five minutes forward and two minutes backward.

"This is not working out, Bob," growled Jennifer.

"Now we take care of business my way. Time for a flying head butt."

Bob tried to help.

"Maybe because raising the hand helps the system push out the waste materials?"

Everyone laughed.

Michael K. scooted his desk toward the window, away from Bob and Jennifer.

"No," said Mrs. Halley firmly. "Raising your hand does not help you push out wastes. But if you have to go to the bathroom, or if you have a question, you must raise your hand."

Bob tried to help some more.

"Maybe if you lift your hand you go faster?"

More laughs.

Michael K. opened his *Giant Collection of Science*

and Facts book and became very interested in reading it, and trying to disappear.

Mrs. Halley felt her head spinning. Why do we raise our hands? What kind of question was that? You might as well ask why the sun comes up in the morning.

Mrs. Halley looked up . . . and saw her answer.

"Goodness' sake. Look at the time. Eleven ten. Class, please close your workbooks and form a line for recess."

The class closed their workbooks and began to line up. Mrs. Halley smiled. The calm of order was restored. No more questions.

Jennifer picked that exact moment to practice her new skill. She raised her hand.

Mrs. Halley could not ignore her own rule.

"Yes, Jennifer?"

"Why?"

"Why what?"

"Why do we form a line?"

Everyone froze.

"Yeah, why do you have to make a line?" asked the big kid.

"Because it's one hundred percent whole grain natural?" said Bob.

The class laughed again. Bob beamed.

"Yes," lied Mrs. Halley. "Now everyone line up."

Michael K. closed his book and got in line as far away from Bob and Jennifer as he possibly could.

Webs

A spider builds its web by connecting main lines of silk with smaller connecting lines.

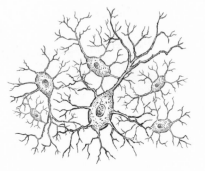

The human brain is a web of cells connected to one another. Thought is a pattern of electrical signals between these cells.

Pudding is pretty much just pudding.

WHAT?
ʃ˙ɑ̊ɫɪ

"**W**hat are you doing?" asked Michael K.

Bob stood behind Michael K. Jennifer stood behind Bob.

"We are following Mrs. Halley's rules," said Bob.

Michael K. turned. Bob turned. Jennifer turned.

Michael K. could not believe this was happening to him.

"You don't stay in line once you are on the playground! Everybody knows that!"

Bob and Jennifer looked

at Michael K. They stayed in line behind him.

Michael K. was about to freak out. This was his worst nightmare ever. Well, one of his worst nightmares. There was that other one with the monster

hiding under his bed. But that was kind of babyish. This was a huge fifth-grade-size nightmare.

Here he was—the very first day of a new school,

just trying to fit in, but somehow already stuck with the two weirdest kids in all of Brooklyn. Everybody in school was going to think he was a weirdo too.

Michael K. sat down next to the chain-link fence. Bob and Jennifer sat down in a line next to him.

"Look," said Michael K. "I don't know where you are from, or what your problem is, but—"

"Yes, we already told you," said Bob. "Remember? We are from planet **SPHDZ**. And our problem is we need to get three point one four million and one Earth persons to become **SPHDZ**."

"Or what?" said Michael K. "Earth gets blown up by giant spaceships with laser cannons? Or melted by an outer-space firestorm? Or smashed by a giant meteor?"

"That would make a great show!" said Jennifer.

"No," said Bob. "None of those things would happen. But if we do not get enough **SPHDZ**, Earth will be turned off."

"And we will not be able to feed on our favorite Earth waves," said Jennifer.

Michael K. tried to make sense of what he had

just heard. His brain felt like pudding. Then a few thoughts fired.

"What do you mean Earth will get turned off?

"And if you really are aliens, what are you doing invading fifth grade?

"And why do you need me?"

"Eeee eee weee," said Bob's pocket. Class hamster Fluffy poked his nose out and crawled onto the top of Bob's head.

"Exactly," said Bob. "You are the leader. You explain Mission **SPHDZ** to Michael K."

Jennifer picked up a stick and chewed it.

Michael K. looked at Major Fluffy.

E ek week," said Major Fluffy.

"Eeeekeeekeeek weeek.

"Week eek eeeekwee weee weee eeee ee eeeek eeeek. Eeek eekeekkeeekee. Ee eee, ee eeek wee week. Eeeek wee eeek eeek weee weeekweek. Weee weee weee! Eeek eek eek, eeek week eek, weeek week week. Week eek wee wee eeekeee, wee weee weee weeeee eek. Wee eeek. Eee weeee. Week eeek eeeekwee weee weee eeee ee eeeek eeeek.

"Eeek eekeekkeeekee. Ee eee, ee eeek wee week. Eeeek wee eeek eeek weee weeekweek. Weee eek eek, eeek week eek, weeek week week. Week eek wee wee eeekeee, wee weee weee weeeee eek.

"Wee eeek. Eee weeee. Week eeek eeeekwee weee weee eeee ee eeek eeeek. Eeek eekeekkeeekee. Ee eee, ee eeek wee week.

"Eeeek wee eeek eeek weee weeekweek. Weee weee. Eeek eek eek, eeek week eek, weeek week week. Week eek wee wee eeekeee, wee weee weee weeeee eek.

"Eee weeee. Week eeek eeeekwee weee weee eeee

ee eeeek eeeek. Eeek eekeekkeeekee. Ee eee, ee eeek wee week. Eeeek wee eeek eeek weee weeekweek. Weee weee weee weeee we.

"Eeek eek eek, eeek week eeek, weeek week week. Week eek wee wee eeekeee, wee weee weee weeeee eek. Wee eeek. Eee weeee.

"Eee eeek, weee weee eeee ee eeeek eeeek. Eeek eekeekkeeekee. Ee eee, ee eeek wee week. Eeeek wee eeek eeek weee weeekweek. Wee eeek. Eee weeee. Week eeek eeeekwee weee weee eeee ee eeeek eeeek. Eeek eekeekkeeekee.

"Ee eee, ee eeek wee week. Eeeek wee eeek eeek weee weeekweek. Weee weee weee! Eeek eek eek, eeek week eeek, weeek week week. Week eek wee wee eeekeee, wee weee weee weeeee eek. Wee eeek. Eee weeee. Week eeek eeeekwee weee weee eeee ee eeeek eeeek.

"Eeek eekeekkeeekee. Ee eee, ee eeek wee week. Weee weee weee. Eeek eek eek, weeek week week. Week eek wee wee eekeee, wee weee weee weeeee eek. Wee eeek. Eee weeee. Week eeek eeeekwee weee weee eeee ee eeeek eeeek."

Fluffy sneezed. He sniffed. Then he continued.

"Ee eee, ee eeek wee week. Eeeek wee eeek eeek weee weeekweek. Weee weee weee! Eeek eek eek, eeek week eeek, weeek week week. Week eek wee wee eekeee, wee weee weee weeeee eek.

"Wee eeek. Eee weeee. Week eeek eeeekwee weee weee eeee ee eeeek eeeek. Eeek eekeekkeeekee. Ee eee, ee eeek wee week. Eeeek wee eeek eeek weee weeekweek. Wee eeek. Eee weeee. Week eeek eeeekwee weee weee, eeee ee eeeek eeeek. Eeek eekeekkeeekee. Ee eee, ee eeek wee week. Eeeek wee eeek eeek weee weeekweek.

"Eeee eee! Eeek eek eek, eeek week eeek, weeek week week. Week eek wee wee eekeee, wee weee weee weeeee eek. Wee eeek.

"Eee weeee.

"Ee eee, ee eeek wee week. Eeeek wee eeek eeek weee weeekweek. Weee weee weee!

"Eeek eek eek, eeek week eeek, weeek week week. Week eek wee wee eeekeee, wee weee weee weeeee eek. Wee eeek. Eee weeee.

"Week eeek eeeekwee weee weee eeee ee eeeek eeeek. Eeek eekeekkeeekee. Ee eee, ee eeek wee week. Eeeek wee eeek eeek weee weeekweek. Wee eeek. Eee weeee. Week eeek eeeekwee weee weee eeee ee eeeek eeeek. Eeek eekeekkeeekee.

"Ee eee, ee eeek wee week. Eeeek wee eeek eeek weee weeekweek. Weee weee weee. Eeek eek eek, eeek week eeek, weeek week week. Week eek wee wee eeekeee, wee weee weee weeeee eek.

"Ee eeek ee eee eek eek weee week."

Major Fluffy paused, then spread out his front paws.

"Eek eeek!"

Chapter 6

WHA–HUH?
Σ ˙ å- ˙˙˙ ˙ ¿

Michael K. stared at Major Fluffy.

Bob and Jennifer stared at Michael K.

"Well?" said Jennifer.

"What do you think, Michael K.?" said Bob. "No artificial flavoring."

"Wha-huh?" said Michael K.

TV and Radio

TV and radio broadcasts travel in waves.

Those waves just keep going and going and going.

One hundred years from now something on a distant planet could be feeding on that Burger King commercial you saw yesterday.

Many Earth persons believe there is an unwritten rule that whenever you really need to find a parking space, you can't find one.

But that is only because most Earth persons don't get around the universe much. If they did, they would know that this is a written rule . . . in every dimension.

And it is strictly enforced.

So when the rusty white van pulled up next to the school yard of P.S. 858, of course there was no parking space for a regulation 1.27 miles.

The driver of the van—a man in faded blue coveralls and very shiny black shoes—stopped the van at a fire hydrant.

Of all days, today he really needed a parking space. And he needed it now. An AEW had been detected at these coordinates. And he needed to be on the ground. Pronto.

The man thought about putting his official AAA card in the van window and parking right here. But that would blow his cover as an AAA ant farmer. Plus, the card never worked anyway. He always got a ticket. Or towed. Or ticketed and then towed. Not good. Either way. He would just sit here and observe. Get the facts. Just the facts.

School. ☑

School playground. ☑

Three funny-looking kids in a line by the fence. ☑

With a hamster. ☑

Kids playing tag. Kids playing kickball. ☑ and ☑

Sand. ☑

Plexiglas. ☑

Tiny little green plastic barn
    and silo and trees. ☑ ☑ ☑

Where could ETs be hiding here? Those extraterres-trials were a sneaky bunch. They could be anywhere. He would have to keep his keen agent eyes open.

Umber stepped out of the van and smacked his head on the van doorframe.

Hard.

"Owwwwww."

Umber saw stars. He saw a giant pro wrestler. He saw a pink unicorn with sparkles.

Wow. That *really* hurt.

Umber closed his eyes and rubbed his head to make it all go away.

Umber wobbled around to the back of the van. He took out his ant-farming tools.

Umber slammed the back door and started across the P.S. 858 playground toward his date with destiny.

Parking or no parking—Umber decided he had to risk it to save the world.

To Protect and to Serve and to Always Look Up.

Umber began practicing the speech he would give to the grateful president of the United States: "It was nothing, sir. Just doing my AAA agent job . . ."

Which is probably why Agent Umber never even saw the pebbly red rubber meteor headed his way.

Waves

Plenty of things move in waves.

Water

Sound

Light

Energy

Ideas?

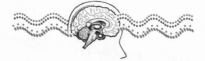

If you could change waves, you could change how something looks, how something sounds, how something . . . thinks?

Chapter 8

YES, I CAN

¥´ß, ^ çå~

"**C**AN YOU HEAR ME NOW?**"** said Bob.

Michael K. shook his head and snapped out of his hamster-listening trance. "What? Yes. Huh? Are you kidding me? What was that?"

Jennifer stood up and started pacing back and forth. "Okay. *LET'S GET IT ON!*"

Michael K. jumped to his feet. "Wait, wait, wait. How did you do that? How did you make it look like the hamster was talking?"

"He does kind of go on and on," said Bob. *"TASTE THE RAINBOW."*

Bob sounded exactly like a Skittles commercial.

"Now you are *really* freaking me out," said Michael K.

"So," said Bob, "you will help us **SPHDZ** three point one four million Earth persons?"

"And one," added Jennifer.

Michael K. looked at Jennifer, then Bob, then Major Fluffy.

The first day of school had just officially gone from bad to worse to crazy town.

A new pattern fired in Michael K.'s brain cells. Michael K. thought:

But that couldn't be real. Michael K.'s brain cells calmed down. They fired in an old, safe, familiar pattern:

"No way," said Michael K. "You are not aliens. There is no such thing as aliens. And if you were, you would have big heads or octopus arms and the flying saucers and laser cannons."

"I told you I should have brought my lasers," said Jennifer.

"No," said Bob. "We talked about that. It makes such a mess."

"Weeee eeeek eeee," said Major Fluffy.

"And that, too," said Bob.

"No way," repeated Michael K., more to himself than to anyone else. "No. Way. If you really are aliens, show me your spaceship or your death ray or something."

"We don't use spaceships," said Bob.

"Of course you don't," said Michael K.

"We change channels," said Jennifer. "It's a simple adjustment of wave forms. Transdimensional slippage. Even Znerfligs can do it. Now come on. *LET'S ROCK!*"

Michael K. did not know what to say.

"We can show you," said Bob. "*YOU ARE IN GOOD HANDS WITH* SPHDZ."

Bob reached into his pocket. He pulled out a small black rectangle with buttons. He held it up to Michael K. "Aha!"

"Very nice," said Michael K.

And then Michael K. formed a plan.

"You have a remote control. Great. Now I completely believe you. Of course you are from outer space. You just wait here, and I will be right back."

"Excellent," said Bob. "**REACH OUT AND TOUCH SOMEONE**."

"*WrestleMania!*" said Jennifer.

"Eeek eeek," said Major Fluffy.

Michael K. began to back away slowly.

Michael K. reviewed his plan. He would

1. tell the yard teacher that Bob and Jennifer were nuts,

2. tell the principal that Bob and Jennifer were nuts, and

3. dial 911 and tell the operator that Bob and Jennifer were nuts.

"I told you Michael K. would **SPHDZ**," said Bob.

"Extreme!" said Jennifer. "Then, can we use our other wave forms?"

Jennifer grabbed the remote. She punched three buttons. And where there had been Jennifer, Bob, and Major Fluffy, the class hamster . . . there was now:

Michael thought:

The wrestler punched the "last" button on the remote.

Jennifer, Bob, and Major Fluffy reappeared.

"Eeee eee eek weeek eee," said Fluffy.

"Oh yeah," said Bob. "And we almost forgot one more thing."

Michael K. did not think he could take one more thing.

Bob added it anyway.

"We must not get caught by the AAA."

CURVE MEETS LINE

Chapter 9!

ç ¨®√´ μ´´†ß ¬^~´

The path traced by a body launched through space is a curve.

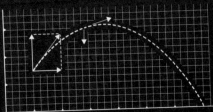

A kickball kicked into the air traces a kickball curve.

The path traced by a body moving along a fixed direction is called a *line*.

An AAA agent walking across a playground traces a line.

The point where a curve crosses a line is called an *intersection*.

But to Agent Umber, the intersection of the kickball curve with his agent line was more of a giant *BOINGK* on his head . . . then darkness.

HOLY COW

·ø¬Ұ ÇøΣ

Chapter 10

U h-huh. Yep. Right. YER OUT!"

The little man in the New York Yankees jacket blew his whistle almost loud enough to break the glass in his extra-large specs.

"BATTER UP!"

A new kicker stepped up to the plate.

"What was that you were saying?"

Michael K. tried to catch the yard teacher's gaze.

Mr. Rizzuto kept his big glasses locked on the kickball game.

"The new kids," repeated Michael K. "There is something really wrong with them."

"Gotta move that runner over. FOUL BALL!"

"They might even be dangerous," said Michael K.

"Pitcher's got a good delivery," said Mr. Rizzuto.

"I think we should tell somebody, like the FBI."

"Reminds me of Seaver."

"Or the CIA."

"Except he's rolling the ball."

"Or—"

"THAT ONE COULD BE OUTTA HERE!
IT'S
GOING,
GOING—oh, jeez!
What is that guy doing walking across the playground? BOOM! He's down! He's out cold! Holy cow! Somebody call the nurse!"

NOT SO SWEET DREAMS

~øt ßø ßƐ¨† ∂®´åµß

Ⓩ

Agent Umber looks around. All he sees is darkness.
Pure inky black deep-space darkness.

Then a tiny, round dot of a planet appears.

The dot grows to a ball, a disk, an enormous circle of

sand, sand, sand.

What is that?

In the distance he sees two giant, flat green trees.

And then the silhouette of a giant green windmill.

Next to it is a green barn. A green bridge. A green house.

Maybe someone is home, Umber thinks. *Maybe someone
can help a lost traveler.* But before Umber can knock, a long

black antenna wiggles out of the ground. The one antenna

is followed by another. The antennae are followed by huge

black pincers, a head, legs, body. . . .

This is no human's farm.

This is a giant ant farm.

The first creature crawls up out of the hole in the sand. More come pouring out. Spindly legs, tapping antennae, clicking pincers everywhere.

Agent Umber tries to run. His legs will barely move. The sand is so hard to run in.

That's when he hears the clicking sound.

The clicking grows louder ... louder ... louder.

Umber's eyes popped open.

A fuzzy giant ant face loomed over him.

"AAIIIIIEEEEEEEEE!"

screamed Umber. "Don't eat me! It is against regulation 837-USZ to eat a federal agent!"

Something cold and rubbery grabbed Umber's head.

"Stop your fussing," said a human voice. The horrible ant creature came into focus as more of a woman with thick, black-framed glasses and a white hat.

The school nurse sat Agent Umber up and checked the bump on his head.

A little man with googly, big glasses and a Yankees jacket stared at him.

School kids surrounded him.

"That's a home run," said the big kid who had kicked the pebbly red ball. "That would have gone to the fence easy if this guy's head hadn't stopped it."

"Holy cow," said the big-glasses guy.

"What?" said Umber.

"I believe you have suffered a concussion. Come along, and you are going to lie down in my sick-room," said the school nurse.

"Thank you, ma'am, but I am on a mission."

"Your only mission right now, Mr. Man, is to get your sick self to my sickroom and lie down."

Agent Umber tried to argue his case.

But no one, on any planet, in any galaxy, ever wins an argument with the school nurse.

Nurse Dominique locked one arm under Umber's arm and escorted him to the P.S. 858 sickroom.

Mr. Rizzuto blew his whistle.

The fifth graders lined up to go back to their classroom.

Michael K. walked right over a card that had fallen out of the AAA ant farmer's repair bag.

AGENT UMBER

AAA

If Found, Contact:
www.antialienagency.com

Electromagnetic Fields

You can't see electromagnetic energy, but the Earth does have a magnetic field. It's like the whole planet is a giant magnet.

Do you think individuals might have their own electromagnetic fields?

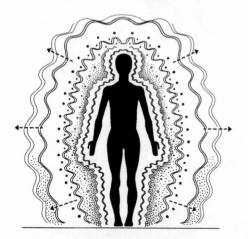

Chapter 12!

IMPRESSIONS
^ µπ® ´ßß^ø˜ß

The rest of the first day of school turned out to be worse than the strange beginning.
A few highlights:

1. Mrs. Halley does not allow changing seats for the first semester. So Michael K. had to move back next to Bob and Jennifer. And Major Fluffy.

2. Reading group buddies are also lunchroom buddies. So Michael K. got to enjoy both *On the Banks of Plum Creek* and chicken nuggets with Bob and Jennifer.

"But what if I already read this last year?" asked Michael K.

"You can read it in English to your reading pals this year," answered Mrs. Halley.

"What part of a chicken is the nuggets?" asked Jennifer.

"People don't usually eat the outside of the banana," said Michael K.

3. Reading group buddies and lunchroom buddies are also computer lab buddies. So Michael K. got to work on another project with the two kids he would most like never to see again.

"Eeek eeek eeek," said Major Fluffy.

"Yes, you are very good at PowerPoint presentations," agreed Bob.

Make that two kids and a hamster he would most like never to see again.

After what seemed like forever, three o'clock finally arrived.

Michael K. had almost convinced himself that the weird thing with the remote and the class hamster hadn't happened, when the dismissal bell rang.

Most of Mrs. Halley's class stuffed their new schoolbooks into their bags and lined up at the door. Jennifer threw two desks down onto the floor and jumped behind them.

The lightbulb in the classroom terrarium popped.

"Those poor meatbags are going to get blasted. Didn't anyone teach them basic cover?"

"Get down, Michael K.!" Bob called from behind Jennifer's desk fort. "That's a Glxxppfff attack signal!"

"It's a dismissal bell," said Michael K. "School is over. It's time to go home. There are no Glxxppfffs around."

What was he saying? Of course there were no Glxxppfffs around. There were no Glxxppfffs anywhere! Michael K. was now totally mental. He had to ditch these crazies.

"Remember your 'Who Is My Neighbor?' homework for

tonight. The questions to help you are on our www .mrshalleyscomets.com website," said Mrs. Halley.

Michael K. squeezed himself to the front of the line. He hustled out the front door and down the high steps, and was almost out the front gate . . . when he heard the voice.

There's one of those voices in every school. It belongs to that kid who bothers everyone. Sometimes the kid is big. Sometimes he is small. Sometimes he is plain looking. Sometimes he is incredibly ugly.

But the voice is always the same. And it's always a bad thing to hear. And it's the worst thing to hear if it is directed at you.

"Ha, ha," said the voice. "You are a Spaceheadz!"

Michael K. kept walking.

"You are a Spaceheadz. The new kid is a Spaceheadz. Spaceheadz. Spaceheadz."

Michael K. stopped. He turned around. Great. The voice was coming from the big, ugly kid in his class. Joey.

Using force was out of the question. So Michael K. tried his only weapon—being agreeable.

"Oh, yeah," said Michael K. "I'm feeling like a Spaceheadz. New school, new neighborhood, new—"

The big kid looked down at Michael K. "No, you dork. You've got 'SPHDZ' written on the side of your book."

Michael K. didn't even have to look. He knew it was probably true. And he had a good guess how it had gotten there.

The big kid punched Michael K.'s social studies book out from under his arm. He started honking again, "Spaceheadz! Spaceheadz! The new kid is a Spaceheadz!"

Now the day was really complete.

Permanently grouped with the weirdos. And picked on by the class bully.

"Spaceheadz! Spaceheadz! The new kid is a—oohhhhhh."

There was a deep sound. A deep sound you couldn't really hear, but could feel in your stomach. Like the deep wave from an underground explosion.

Joey's eyes crossed, and he quit making his honking noises. He wobbled around and tried not to fall over.

Jennifer picked up Michael K.'s social studies textbook and put it back under his arm.

"Had to stop the bad waves coming out of that kid," said Jennifer. "Total **SMACKDOWN**."

"Uh, yeah. Thanks," said Michael K. He picked up the papers that had fallen out of his social studies book. He didn't know it, but he also picked up a card that had blown across the playground.

Boom, Bwee, Eeek

Elephants communicate by making sounds below the level of human hearing. These sounds are called subsonic.

Whales also communicate with sound waves, sonic and subsonic.

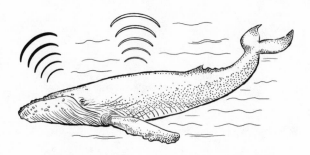

Ants communicate with smells.

Dog barks, squirrel chatter, pigeon coos, and hamster eeks are sound waves too.

M ichael K. turned to walk home. Bob and Jennifer followed him.

Michael K. turned around and walked the other direction down the street. Bob and Jennifer followed him.

"Okay," said Michael K. "Good-bye. Now you go to your house. I go to my house." *And then I will tell my mom and dad that I have to go to a different school . . . any school,* thought Michael K.

"So, you are a **SPHDZ** too, Michael K.," said Bob. "That is fantastic!"

"No," said Michael K.

"Now we must collect supplies," said Jennifer.

"No," said Michael K.

"I AM CUCKOO FOR COCOA PUFFS," said Bob.

"And **AJAX IS STRONGER THAN DIRT,"** added Jennifer.

Michael K. didn't know what to say.

He tried to decide the best way to escape. Should he be mean to Bob and Jennifer? Should he yell at them? Or should he just run away as fast as possible?

Bob bent down to pat a fire hydrant. "So cute," said Bob.

"Why do your little Earth people wheel around little pretend Earth people?" asked Jennifer. She walked over toward a little kid pushing a doll in a stroller.

Michael K. turned around to run, when a large black dog with one white ear walked up to them.

"Woof," barked the dog.

"Woof woof," barked the dog, staring intently at Bob's shirt pocket.

"Weeek eeek," said Bob's pocket.

"Wooof woof woof. Bark bark. Yap yap yap."

Major Fluffy stuck his head out of Bob's pocket.

"Eek eeek eeek-week."

"Woof."

"Eeek."

The dog ran off.

Michael K. stared.

"What?" said Major Fluffy. "You don't speak Dog, either?"

NO ESCAPE
~ø ´ßçåп´

Chapter 14!

"M a'am? My shoes? Could I have my shoes back? I just polished them this morning."

"All in good time, mister. When your head is better. Now get yourself back in the sickroom and lie down."

"I probably should not reveal this information to you. It's highly classified. But I am a federal agent, ma'am. AAA. Here on a possible AEW. Should not be lying down on a cot in the school nurse's office. Safety of the world. In my hands right now."

"Now I know you are still suffering, poor man. Still talking your crazy talk about little men from outer space. Don't you worry. Nurse Dominique will know when you are better and ready to go home."

"But—"

"No buts about it, Mr. Umber. Take these two aspirin and lie down quietly."

"Yes, Nurse Dominique."

"And what kind of name is that? Umber. Where are your people from? Giving you a funny name like that."

"I think I'll take these two aspirin and lie down quietly."

If you look up the word "shock" on dictionary.com, one definition reads "a sudden or violent disturbance of the mind."

But that really isn't enough of a word to describe Michael K.'s mental disintegration. "Mind bomb" is more like it. Or maybe "world smash." Or "blaawaaawaaawaaawaaa."

Michael K. stared at Major Fluffy and tried to understand a talking hamster. He tried to still believe that Bob and Jennifer and Fluffy were not from another planet.

He couldn't do either.

Michael K.'s feet decided what to do before his brain did.

They started running.

Michael K. ran down the block and across the street.

Bob and Jennifer ran down the block. They didn't seem to notice the light change.

They ran across the street.

One car screeched to a stop and honked its horn.

Jennifer made the exact same honking sound back.

Michael K. stopped running and looked back.

Now Jennifer and Bob were standing in the middle of the street. Now moms picking up their little kids, and the crossing guard down the block, were watching. A giant

DON'T
LITTER

red truck was speeding right toward Bob and Jennifer. And they were not moving. At all.

Michael K. knew that they were not planning to move.

Michael K.'s fast feet and kind heart took over before his brain did. Again.

Michael K. dropped his books, raced into the street,

and scooped Jennifer and Bob (and Major Fluffy) out of the way.

The giant red truck raced by, blasting its air horn.

Jennifer made an air-horn honk noise back. Bob waved.

"That was the real thing!" said Bob.

Michael K. was freaked out. "You almost got flattened! Haven't you ever seen a traffic light?"

"Traffic light?" said Bob.

"See that light up there? And then the light sign down there? The little walking man means 'walk.' The

hand means 'don't walk.'"

"I understand," said Bob. "Now we are totally like regular Earth persons.

Little walking man, walk. Hand, don't walk."

"You guys really *are* from outer space," said Michael K.

Now a whole crowd of kids and parents and drivers were staring at them.

"Come on," said Michael K. "Let's get out of here."

"Yes," said Bob. "We know where to go to get everything we need. The dog earthling told us to go garbage, garbage, tree. Lamppost, lamppost, fire hydrant."

"What?" said Michael K. "Oh, forget it. Come on." Michael K. walked down the sidewalk.

A tow truck pulled away a rusty white van illegally parked next to a fire hydrant.

"Stop!" yelled Bob.

Bob and Jennifer stood frozen like statues.

"What? What?" said Michael K.

Bob pointed. "The little hand."

"Don't walk," said Jennifer.

"Oh, man," said Michael K.

Chapter 16

THERE'S A MAN

†˙˙®´æß   å   µå˜

A man in blue coveralls tiptoed down the empty school hallway. The shiny green linoleum felt slippery. Very slippery in stocking feet.

There's a man who leads a life of danger.

To everyone he meets he stays a stranger.

With something something makes, another
  something something takes.

Something something else about tomorrow.

"'Secret agent man,'" sang Agent Umber, not realizing that he was now singing out loud. "'Secret agent man! They've given you a number and taken away your—'"

"Mr. Umber?" a stern voice called from the empty sickroom.

Agent Umber did not hesitate.

He ran.

He ran down the slippery hallway.

He ran down the rough and pebbly stairs.

He ran out the school doors, across the playground, and over to an empty space next to a fire hydrant where there used to be a rusty white van with an AAA ANT FARMING sign on its side.

Agent Umber wondered why this never happened to Secret Agent Man.

"Mr. Umber?" The stern voice cut across the playground. "I know who you are. I will be looking for you."

"'They've given you a number,'" sang Umber, hop-running down the sidewalk in stocking feet, "'and taken away your name.'"

HEAVEN
· ´ å √ ´ ˜

"OOOOOOOOOOHHHHHHHH!" moaned Bob, standing next to the rows of paper towels.

"WOWWWWWWWW!" yelled Jennifer, down near the bleach and laundry detergent.

And that wasn't even embarrassing compared with what had happened on the way to the supermarket.

Major Fluffy had talked to three more dogs, a squirrel, and two pigeons.

Bob had fallen in love with a purple Dora the Explorer backpack and hugged two more fire hydrants and three parking meters.

And Jennifer had tried to eat a flower, a Peanut M&M's "Melts in your mouth, not in your hands" wrapper, and a Dr Pepper "Makes the world taste better" can.

The three dogs, squirrel, and pigeons directed them to the Key Food grocery store. This was getting stranger by the minute.

If the Spaceheadz mission was a plot to take over the world, what were they planning to do? Clean it? Mop it up?

Because right now Bob and Jennifer were jumping around filling a shopping cart with laundry detergent and paper towels.

And why did they need Michael K.?

"TWICE THE POWER!"

"THE QUICKER PICKER-UPPER!"

Standing in the cleaning-products aisle, Michael K. realized that he was in deep trouble. This morning he had only been worried about fitting in at his new school. Now he was worried that three Spaceheadz were going to use him to take over the world. With paper towels and detergent.

"Yes!" Bob called. "Charmin! We must also use this. It is ultrastrong! And it also makes bears very happy."

Michael K. took the Charmin from Bob. "What? No. This is toilet paper! What are you talking about?"

"It makes bears happy," said Bob. "We will use it to make Earth persons happy and want to be **SPHDZ**."

Michael K. held the package of Charmin Ultra Strong and looked at the drawing of a bear holding a strip of toilet paper. He did look pretty happy.

"Well, it doesn't have anything to do with bears," said Michael K. "It's toilet paper, you know?"

"Yes—we know we must have it because it is ultra-strong!" said Jennifer.

Michael K. was wondering how to explain toilet paper, when the girl with the jet-black hair, the one from Mrs. Halley's class, walked around the corner.

"Oh, hey. Aren't you the new kids in class? I'm Venus. Venus Chang."

"TJ," said the comic-artist kid with Venus.

"And these two monsters are our little brothers, Hugo and Willy. They are in the same kindergarten. We have to get them home every day."

Hugo and Willy started crawling around on the floor making monster noises.

"Monsters?" said Jennifer. She threw her Dial "Aren't you glad you use Dial?" soap on the floor. "We must crush them before they destroy everything!"

"We have seen it happen," said Bob.

Michael K. grabbed Jennifer. "It's okay. Venus and TJ will take care of the monsters. Please don't crush them."

"Eeek a week eek," said Fluffy.

"You have a hamster just like the one in class!" said Venus.

Michael K. tried to hide the toilet paper, hold back Jennifer, and smile all at once.

"Oh, yeah," he said brilliantly.

"And what about you?" said Venus Chang.

"Huh?" said Michael K.

"That's a funny name, Huh."

"Oh, no. I mean my name is Michael K."

Venus eyed the whole group . . . and their cart full of toilet paper and detergent and paper towels.

"You guys are very funny. Where are you all from?"

Bob started to say, "SPH—"

"Oh, we are not from the same place," said Michael K., cutting off Bob. "At all. And we're not really friends. I was just helping Bob and Jennifer get some . . . uh . . . supplies. Because they don't really know much about how we do things, you know?"

"Like they don't have stores in Bulgaria?"

"Right," said Michael K.

"Need more **SPHDZ**," said Jennifer.

Little Hugo looked at Jennifer. "You sound funny."

The metal shopping cart rolled by itself and stuck to Jennifer's leg . . . like it was a magnet.

"What are Spaceheadz?" said Willy. "I use toilet paper. When I sit on the potty—"

Lucky for Michael K., Venus's phone rang. Hannah Montana's "Best of Both Worlds." Venus looked at the text on her pink rhinestone-covered phone.

"Ooooooh," said Bob.

"Oops," said Venus. "Gotta go. Come on, monsters."

Venus and TJ rounded up their little brothers, who were now meowing like cats in front of Tony the Tiger on the Frosted Flakes boxes.

Venus waved. "See you tomorrow."

Venus, TJ, Willy, and Hugo disappeared around the giant display of Ajax, "Stronger than dirt."

"See you tomorrow," copied Bob.

"Wow," said Fluffy. "She can see us in the future!"

Chapter 18

RING, RING
®^~©, ®^~©

"Three, four."

"Shut the door."

"More alien energy waves detected in section B-5. B-5."

Agent Umber checked his mobile AAA Coordinate Decoder®.

"I'm on it, Chief," said Umber.

"Umber, did you make contact at D-7 this morning? We lost you."

"Definite contact, Chief."

"Did you use your head this time, Umber?"

"Definitely, Chief."

"Well, go check the new AEW spike at B-5. I do not want Washington to hear anything about this."

Umber juggled his decoder and map. He located B-5.

"Oh, raspberries," said Umber. "First I have to get my van out of the pound."

"What was that, Umber?"

"I, uh, have to see a man about a hound."

And at just that moment a black dog with a white ear trotted over. He raised one leg. He squirted on Umber's left sock.

"Oh, Pop-Tarts!" yelled Umber.

The dog gave Umber a funny look . . . then walked away.

"What is going on there, Umber?"

"Nothing, Chief. I've got it all under control. But I think I might just need a new pair of shoes."

"Form SH-748/002.RE. You need to download it from antialienagency.com. Fill it out in triplicate. Everything must go through E5. You know that."

Umber did know that. But E5 was where Umber had been given his Picklephone®, his Stove Radio®, and his Houseplant PottyPal®.

Umber tried his best to avoid E5.

"And Umber?"

"Yes, Chief."

"What's wrong with the shoes you've got?"

Umber paused. He crinkled his map next to his phone.

"Losing . . . nection . . . can . . . will . . . erk . . . ga . . ."

Agent Umber closed his Picklephone®.

Agent Umber jogged toward the car pound to retrieve his van.

Agent Umber left a trail of soggy dog-pee sock prints.

STRONGER, WHITER, LONGER-LASTING

ßt®ø~©´®, Σ´^†´®,
¬ø~©´®-¬åßt^~©

Ⓩ

Have you ever heard that expression "Things are spinning out of control"? Because Michael K. thought that was a very good description of what was happening in the Key Food store.

Bob smeared Crest Extra Whitening toothpaste on his arms and forehead.

Jennifer snacked on a handful of Fresh Step maximum odor control kitty litter.

Fluffy looked through two Cheerios.

And all three Spaceheadz had wrapped an arm (or a hamster leg) in toilet paper.

Their grocery cart was now full of Tide detergent, Charmin toilet paper, Old Spice deodorant, Bounty paper towels, and Gillette shaving cream.

"Most excellent supplies," said Jennifer.

"Now we are stronger, whiter, and longer-lasting," said Bob.

"Why me?" said Michael K.

"Because Michael K. **CAN DO ANYTHING**," said Jennifer.

And that's when Michael K. really freaked out. Because that's when Jennifer held up a box of that cereal—with the picture Michael K.'s dad had sworn no one would ever see. That lame picture and lame ad slogan that could ruin him for life:

Michael K. started waving his arms around. He did that when he was excited.

Michael K. was very excited. He was also annoyed, and upset, and freaked out, and mad.

He grabbed the SuperCrunchies.

"Okay, how did you find out about this?"

Blackmail. That had to be it. If he didn't cooperate, the new kids. . . or aliens. . . or whatever they were . . . were going to show this embarrassment to everyone.

This could not happen.

"We saw your broadcast. All **SPHDZ** saw your broadcast," said Bob. "You can do anything. You can help us get three point one four million and one Earth people to be **SPHDZ**, and make the Total **SPHDZ** Brain Wave."

Michael K. held his head in his hands.

Michael K. tried again to organize his thoughts into a pattern that made some kind of sense. They suddenly made a terrible sense.

"Wait a minute, wait a minute. Wait. A. Minute. Let me get this straight. On your planet you saw the commercial of me eating SuperCrunchies?"

"Yes."

"And saying I can do anything?"

"Yes."

"So now you actually think I can do anything?"

"Yes."

"We have learned everything about your planet by feeding on your broadcast waves," said Bob.

"That is how we look so natural as Earth persons," added Jennifer.

"Oh," said Michael K., feeling a bit sick. He also

had a feeling that this was going to really mess up his fifth-grade year.

"And why are we getting Charmin?"

"Because it is ultrastrong!"

"And Ajax?"

"STRONGER THAN DIRT!"

Jennifer picked up a six-pack of Budweiser and dropped it in the cart. "We can also use the king of beers!"

"No, no, no!" said Michael K. He took the beer out of the cart and grabbed the shaving cream too. "We are ten years old. We can't buy beer."

"Michael K. is right," said Bob. "The king of beers is for large Earth animals. I think they are called horses."

Michael K. stared at Bob.

Michael K. realized that the Spaceheadz believed everything they saw on TV and in ads. Michael K. realized he was in a lot of trouble. Michael K.

decided he had to do something drastic.

"Okay," said Michael K. "I am going to take care of everything."

"Michael K. can *do* anything!" yelled Bob.

"But please stop saying that."

Jennifer licked the top of an Old Spice High Endurance deodorant stick. "Mmm-mmm. Fresh. *LONG-LASTING.*"

"Eeek eee, ee eek?" asked Fluffy.

"Oh, yes," answered Bob. "Because if Michael K. does not help us, Earth will definitely be turned off."

Michael K. backed away slowly. He had a new plan. Get away. Open his cell phone. Dial 911. And get some help!

Michael K. turned and ran—right into a very large lady dressed all in white.

Nurse Dominique—because yes, it was her—
took one look at Michael K., the six-pack of Budweiser, and the streams of toilet paper.

"What in the world?!"

Interference/Amplification

Waves that are not in sync interfere with each other and make a smaller wave.

Destructive interference

Waves that are in sync amplify each other and make a bigger wave.

Constructive interference

THE PLOT THICKENS
†·´ ⊓¬ø† †·ˆç°´~ß

Chapter 20!

A grocery cart.

   Items:

1. Charmin Ultra Strong

2. Ajax, "Stronger than dirt"

3. Old Spice High Endurance

4. And some other off-brand cereal? Super Something?

Some would see everyday purchases.

But others, looking through the trained eyes of an AAA agent, looking through binoculars, looking through branches and leaves of a tree, might see something very different.

A plot.

A plot to invade Earth and mess up the republic for which it stands, one nation, under God, with liberty and justice for all.

What was going on with these kids? Every time he got an AEW report, these kids were at the location.

Aha! That was it.

The kids must be chasing the aliens too!

Umber had heard about these other alien chasers. Nothing but glory hounds. This could be trouble. If they caught the aliens, they would get all of the credit. And Umber would be busted down to the bottom ranks of the AAA. Again.

Agent Umber shifted his weight on the tree branch he was perched on.

He didn't hear the faint crack.

The kid with the book bag was holding the funny cereal, waving his arms around, walking back and forth. Very excited about something. He was probably the leader.

The girl in the funny dress and the boy in the pink shirt were just standing there. Listening. Following his orders. No threat.

But where were the aliens?

And what were those kids up to with toilet paper, breakfast cereal, cleanser, and deodorant?

Agent Umber lowered his binoculars and used all of his agent-smarts to figure out what kind of plot this could be.

Agent Umber couldn't think of anything good.

So he looked back through his binoculars. The view was all white. Focus. A white dress, a white cap, white shoes . . .

Her!

Umber jumped up. He jumped back. He forgot he was in a tree.

So the branch that had faintly cracked a little earlier didn't break.

But Agent Umber did step back into thin air.

And because he was not a cartoon character, he didn't have time to look around and then look down. He didn't have time to make a face or hold up a sign.

He just dropped ten feet and landed flat on his back on the roof of a familiar battered white van, recently out of the NYC car pound.

The van's new sign said:

AAA
TREE TRIMMING

The boom of the denting van roof didn't attract much attention on busy Fifth Avenue.

But it did knock a certain federal agent unconscious for the second time that day.

Chapter 21

YES, MA'AM

Ɏ´ß, µåæåµ

Michael K. tried to warn Nurse Dominique about the Spaceheadz and about their plan to take over the world.

He really did.

"I don't know what you children are up to, messing around in the grocery store. But I am your school nurse, and I will help you. So first you will pick up every bit of this mess."

"But—," said Michael K.

"No buts about it, young man."

Bob and Jennifer did exactly what Nurse Dominique told them to do.

Michael K. picked up a SuperCrunchies box. He whispered to Nurse Dominique, "I think they are—"

"I think you are about to test my patience. You are the new children in Mrs. Halley's class, aren't you?"

"Yes, ma'am."

"So you will clean up this mess. You will stop this foolishness. And I will take you home before you get into any serious trouble. Understood?"

Michael K. tried to say, "But these two kids and their hamster are from another planet and they are crazy and they are going to mess up my whole life . . . and maybe turn off the whole planet. Help!"

But when Michael K.'s eyes met Nurse Dominique's eyes, he ended up saying only one word.

"Understood."

CLEANUP IN AISLE FIVE

Chapter 22!

ç¬´å̃¨π ^~ å̂ß¬´ ƒ^√´

A grocery delivery guy in blue coveralls with the logo "AAA Grocery Delivery" stood rubbing the bump on his head, holding a box of Kellogg's Frosted Flakes.

What could it mean?

The facts. Just the facts.

It had been a box of Kellogg's Frosted Flakes.

But now it was a box of Frosted SPHDZ.

And this.

It had been an eight-pack of Charmin Ultra Strong.

But now it was eight rolls of SPHDZ Ultra Strong.

And no telling what this was.

Was it part of the AEW?

Who were these aliens? What kind of invasion was this?

Agent Umber peeled the ragged **SPHDZ** sticker off the Frosted Flakes box and examined it with all of his agent powers.

"Oh, so here's the wise guy plastering his stickers on my merchandise." A round man in a Key Food shirt came barreling down the aisle.

"Who? Wha? Me?" said Umber, holding the Frosted Flakes box in one hand and the **SPHDZ** sticker in the other.

"No, the guy behind you. Sheesh. YEAH, I'm talking to you, AAA Groceries! What is this? Some kind of new ad campaign? What the heck is SPHDZ?"

Umber stammered, "Uh . . . I—"

"You know what? I don't care. You better just get those stickers off my cereal, off my toilet paper, off my beer, and off anything else you've put them on in my store!"

"Oh, no, there's been a mistake."

"You better believe there's been a mistake, Mr. AAA. It was your mistake to come in here and SPHDZ my groceries in my store!"

Umber flashed his badge. "I am—"

"I don't need any help with my car. And you are in big trouble if I have to call your supervisor!"

Umber thought about this. The little, round man was completely wrong. But he was also completely right. The chief did not need to hear about this.

"So, are you going to clean up? Or do I have to make that call?"

"Not a problem, sir."

Agent Umber peeled a sticker off SPHDZ Cap'n Crunch.

He fixed a box of "Snap, crackle, pop" SPHDZ Krispies.

He cleaned up SPHDZ, "Breakfast of champions."

He unstickered SPHDZ Ultra Strong, SPHDZ Ultra Soft, all-temperature SPHDZ, extra-strength SPHDZ, SPHDZ Lite, SPHDZ Dark, whole wheat SPHDZ, organic SPHDZ, new and improved SPHDZ.

He restored safe, effective, original, longer, sweeter, proven, fresher, low-sodium, back-to-school, extra-thick, as-advertised, revolutionary, recycled, and some-assembly-required SPHDZ.

He wondered what this SPHDZ meant.

And then he started on aisle four.

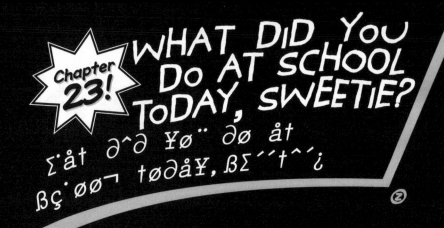

Chapter 23! WHAT DID YOU DO AT SCHOOL TODAY, SWEETIE?

The question hung over Michael K. like a sword—pointy end down.

But it's the question that doesn't really have an answer.

It's a question like, What is the sound of one hand clapping? Or, What is the smell of the color green?

Which is exactly why it is so hard to answer.

"Uh . . . I don't know," said Michael K., in a brilliant reply, just as classic as the question itself.*

Michael K. stuffed a piece of chicken and a blob of mashed potatoes into his mouth to stall for more time.

What did he do at school today? What didn't he do at school today?

*The other classic being "Nothing."

He might have met three invaders from outer space who had learned (and believed) everything they knew from TV. He might have talked to a hamster. And he might have found out that if he didn't help sign up 3,140,001 earthlings as Spaceheadz, Earth would be turned off, whatever that meant.

Before Michael K. could swallow, more questions followed.

"How was your teacher?"

"What are your classmates like?"

"Did you make any new friends?"

"Do you have any homework?"

Baby K. banged her mini spoon on her high-chair tray.

"Ahh ahh, goo goo, gar oooooh?"

Michael K. smiled. His baby sister's question was the easiest to answer. "Yes. And we also goo goo blarb blarbed."

Baby K. laughed.

Mom and Dad K. looked at Michael K., waiting for an answer.

Michael K. swallowed hard. He realized he couldn't be a baby. He was a fifth grader. He would have to face this like an adult.

Or at least like a fifth grader.

"I did meet some other new kids today," said Michael K. "And they were really weird. I think they are from another planet."

Dad K. took some more mashed potatoes. Mom K. nodded. "Kids who grow up in different places can seem very different. Just like some of the people in my new assignment here in New York."

"No," said Michael K. "They are not different like your new work people. They are different like they really are from another planet. And they saw me on the Super-

Crunchies commercial. And they want me to help them put together three million Spaceheadz."

"One of our best ad campaigns ever," said Dad K. "That must still be on the air in some of the out-markets. Fantastic."

"No," said Michael K. "That is not fantastic. Because they saw me in that lame SuperCrunchies costume, they think I . . . well, if we don't sign up . . . I mean, this could be the end of the world!"

Mom K. wiped some stray chicken gravy off Baby K.'s chin. "Learning how to make friends in a new place is tricky. It might seem like the end of the world."

"How is your teacher?" asked Dad K. again.

Michael K.'s head almost exploded.

What was going on? It was like he was speaking Hamster or something. Why couldn't he get anyone to believe him? Or even listen to him?

Michael K. pounded on his social studies book. "They are aliens. They are going to ruin my life."

The dinner table was suddenly very quiet.

"Now, that is just about enough," said Mom K. "I'm sure your first day of school was a bit stressful. But there is no need to pound on the table."

"Why don't you take a time-out," said Dad K. "Go to your room. Do your homework."

"Fine," said Michael K.

He scooped up his books and made as much noise as he could stomping up the steps. When they came begging him to save the world, he would send them to their room.

"Ahh," said Baby K. "Ah gaaah."

And you have no idea how right she was.

Aspen Trees

The largest organism on the planet Earth is not

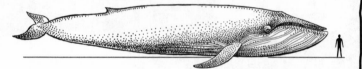

It is not

It is this bunch of aspen trees in Utah.

Above ground, the trees look like separate plants.

But below ground, they are all connected by a single root system.

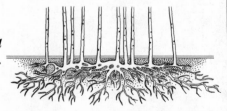

Broken toaster, rusty eggbeater, ceramic angel, incense sticks, fake-wood-paneled cassette tape player, statue of Saint George killing a dragon, *Little Mermaid* video, three dusty

glass bottles labeled SMOLTZ DAIRY, shoe box full of knobs and buttons, plastic salt and pepper shakers shaped like penguins, twelve copies of *National Geographic* magazine

from April 1989 to March 1990, He-Man action figure, framed picture of 2002 New York Mets, four metal Matchbox cars, purple-haired pink Princess Sparkle My Little Pony, slightly rusted spatula with a long wooden handle, half-bald battery-operated monkey in a clown suit holding two cymbals, green glass Coke bottle, broken silver pocket watch, and one shoe box full of picture postcards from around the world.

These were some of the treasures for sale on the table in front of the red brick building of Mr. and Mrs. Rodriguez.

On the right side of the Rodriguezes' red brick building was a bar with a neon sign that spelled out its name: JACKIE's 5ᵀᴴ AMENDMENT.

On the left side of the Rodriguezes' red brick building was a door with **SPHDZ**.

Two kids stepped out of a black Ford Crown Victoria.

"Understood?" asked the driver.

"Yes, ma'am," said Bob.

"Yes, ma'am," echoed Jennifer.

"Eeek week," added Fluffy.

"All right, then," said Nurse Dominique. "No more foolishness. I will see you at school tomorrow morning." Then she drove off in her Crown Vic.

That's when Bob and Jennifer saw Mr. Rodriguez's table of treasures.

"Ooooooooh!!"

Bob held up the small, chubby, long-haired pink plastic version of a pony. "I can't believe it."

Jennifer scooped up a greasy, clamshell-shaped appliance.

"An Inter-Z wave transponder? How long have your people had this tech?" Jennifer asked Mr. Rodriguez.

"Five dollars for both," said Mr. Rodriguez from his lawn chair.

"Aren't you the new kids who moved next door?" asked Mrs. Rodriguez.

"Yes," said Bob. "We have Charmin Ultra Strong and SuperCrunchies! Nurse Dominique got them for us."

"Primitive power sourcing. Yet fully operational," said Jennifer. "Yes, we will be needing this, and also"—Jennifer picked up the eggbeater—"your directional receiver." Jennifer grabbed the Matchbox cars. "And these."

"You kids aren't from around here, are you?" asked Mrs. Rodriguez.

"Neighbor special, little amigos. Everything you want—five dollars," said Mr. Rodriguez.

Bob remembered Nurse Dominique giving the people at Key

Food pieces of green paper for the Charmin and SuperCrunchies.

Bob put down his Charmin, his SuperCrunchies, and his Princess Sparkle My Little Pony.

Fluffy popped his head out and saw the monkey.

"Eeek eek. Wee eee."

"Oh, yes!" said Jennifer.

Jennifer got very excited.

The half-bald monkey clapped his cymbals. The second hand of the broken watch spun around its dial. Mr. Rodriguez jumped back from his table of treasures.

"Aiyee, Mami!"

Bob tore five pieces of paper from his notebook. He drew

faces and numbers on them. He handed them to Mr. Rodriguez.

"Have a nice day."

Bob and Jennifer and Fluffy picked up all of their treasures and walked into their **SPHDZ** door.

The monkey and the watch hand stopped.

"Those kids are definitely not from around here," said Mrs. Rodriguez.

"That's for sure," said Mr. Rodriguez.

He looked inside the cymbal-clapping monkey just to double-check what he knew for sure.

Sí. No batteries. *Nada*.

Mr. Rodriguez carefully filled the newly empty space on his treasure table by moving the penguins a bit to the left and the Coke bottle a bit to the right.

"And I never seen nobody so excited about a George Foreman grill."

Michael K. stomped up the stairs, stomped into his room, threw his books on his bed, and plopped down at his desk.

Time-out. What kind of babyish punishment was that? They would be sorry when the whole Earth got turned off because the one guy who could save the world was having a time-out.

But what was he going to do now? Where could he go for help?

What had Bob said on the playground? It was that "one more thing."

"We must not get caught by the AAA."

Maybe the AAA could help him get rid of the Spaceheadz.

Michael K. turned on his computer.

He Googled "AAA." A bunch of auto, and accounting, and astronomy sites turned up. No help at all.

He tried Wikipedia. More AAA garbage. Nothing about aliens.

Michael K. clicked around, watched a couple YouTube skateboard videos, checked out his favorite skate shop site. Vans, Adidas, Nike shoes. Element, Mystery, Flip decks. And what used to be his favorite company for everything—Alien Workshop.

Now the Alien Workshop Dyrdek Soldier X Band deck, with its picture of a giant alien face, was just freaking him out.

"Might as well do my stupid homework," Michael K. said to no one but himself.

He went to www.mrshalleyscomets.com.

What a goofy-looking website.

Michael K. clicked on "homework assignments."

- Complete the "Who Is My Neighbor?" paper.
- Read chapter 1 of *On the Banks of Plum Creek*.

- Read pages 9-12 of chapter 2, "Our Country's Regions," in our social studies textbook. Answer questions 3, 4, and 7 at the end of the chapter.

"Great," said Michael K.

Michael K. picked his social studies book up off his bed. He opened it, and there it was. The answer to his Spaceheadz problem:

Chapter 26

NO ALIEN

~ø å¬^´~

Michael K. clicked around antialienagency.com.
Lots of mottoes and eagles and stars and
arrows. Lots of stuff about protecting the world.
This was the real thing. But there didn't seem to be
any way to get into the "Top Secret Agent" part
of the site without a password.

There was a tab called "Report an Alien Sight-
ing." Michael K. clicked it.

A phone number.

Yes! It was now or never.

Michael K. dialed the number.

One ring. Two rings. Three rings.

"Hello. You have reached the AAA hotline. If

you are calling to report an alien abduction—press, or say, one. If you are calling to report possible alien contact—press, or say, two. If you are calling to report ghosts, don't be silly. There is no such thing as ghosts. Press zero to repeat your options."

Michael K. pressed two.

"Thank you. You have reached the Alien Contact Center. Please hold your phone near your alien, then press the star key so that an agent may locate you."

Downstairs the front doorbell rang. Michael K. could hear his mom opening the door and talking to someone.

"Arrr!" said Michael K. in frustration. "The aliens don't live with me. I just want to report them and get rid of them!"

"I do not understand your response. Please hold your phone near your alien, then press the star key so that an agent may locate you."

"Arr!"

"I do not underst—"

Michael K. snapped his phone shut. "How am I supposed to hold my phone near them?"

Footsteps up the stairs. A knock on Michael K.'s door. Mom K. opened the door and peeked in.

"Michael, sweetie. Your new friends are here."

"New friends?" said Michael K.

"Bob and Jennifer," said Mom K. "They said you are working on a project together? They seem like nice kids. They brought along their hamster."

The world turned. Michael K. formed a new plan. How was Michael K. going to report the aliens and get his normal fifth-grade life back?

"Oh, right," said Michael K.

That's how.

WATCH

Σåtç˙

Mrs. Halley sat quietly in her red and gold living-room chair. She did not move. Her book, *The Joy of Labradoodles*, lay open in her lap.

Her eyes were closed.

So Mrs. Halley did not see, or hear, the Channel 11 News Team cover the "rash of strange electrical happenings in Brooklyn today."

And she would not be awake for "more news at ten," either.

Baby K. sat quietly in her Fisher-Price Think Pink bouncer. She watched the baby face in the middle of the sun rise over the Teletubbies' world.

The baby sun laughed and said, "Goo oooh ooh goo."

Baby K. laughed and answered, "Ooh goo."

ONE SLICE—WITH MUSHROOMS AND PENCILS

Chapter 28!

ø˜´ ß¬ˆç´−Σˆ†˙
µ¨ß˙®øøµß å˜∂ π´˜ç^¬ß

Ⓩ

Mom K. opened the door a little wider. Bob and Jennifer and Fluffy piled into Michael K.'s bedroom.

Jennifer picked a new pencil up off Michael K.'s desk.

Bob galloped a pink My Little Pony across Michael K.'s bed.

"Weeee eeee eeeek," said Fluffy.

"See?" said Michael K. to Mom K. "I told you they were from another planet. Just look at them!"

But Mom K. had already closed the door and was half-way down the stairs.

Bob picked up a comic from Michael K.'s desk. "Michael K. is friends with Spider-Man!"

Jennifer pulled some kind of contraption out of Bob's Dora backpack. She unfolded it and pointed an eggbeater out the window.

Fluffy jumped around the teddy bear keyboard, typing out:

"Wait, wait, wait," said Michael K. "What are you doing?"

"We are so **READY TO RUMBLE**," said Jennifer.

Michael K. looked at the screen. "But what is this? What did you do?"

"We are getting SPHDZ out there," said Bob. "We have made a beautiful SPHDZ website to sign up a whole swarm of Earth persons."

"SPHDZ . . . pay-per-view," said Jennifer.

"**GOT SPHDZ**?" added Bob.

"Eeee eek ee we weeek," said Fluffy.

"Yes," said Bob. "And Fluffy is thinking about starting a blog."

Michael K. could only stare. He felt his phone in his pocket. He had to turn these Spaceheadz in—quick. But he had to get them someplace where they couldn't be connected with him or his family. He had to get them somewhere out of his house.

"I've got it," said Michael K.

Bob brushed the purple hair on his My Little Pony. "What is 'it'?" asked Bob. "More plans for SPHDZ?"

"Yes," said Michael K. "More plans for Spaceheadz. We have to go get some pizza. Down at the pizza place."

That's where Michael K. could make the call and get rid of his Spaceheadz problem once and for all.

"Walk," said Michael K. Then he led Bob, Jennifer, and Major Fluffy downstairs to the front door.

"We're going down the block for a slice of pizza," Michael K. called to Mom and Dad K.

"You growing kids eat every five minutes," said Mom K.

"PIZZA, PIZZA," said Bob.

And Michael K. led the Spaceheadz to their end.

Flocks and Schools and Swarms

Birds gather in flocks.

Fish form schools.

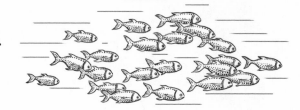

Bees make swarms.

Sticking together, they improve their chances of survival by confusing and scaring bigger predators.

Flocks and schools and swarms also look very cool.

Chapter 29

BZZZT

∫ΩΩΩ†

U mber's Picklephone® vibrated and buzzed.

Text message from AAA HQ.

Agent Umber leaped into action.

He forgot he was sitting in the back of his AAA van. Bam! went his head on the dented metal roof.

He didn't see pink unicorns and wrestlers this time.

But he did see stars and black floating spots.

Umber sat back down at his mobile control center.

This was it.

He would, carefully, take action.

Chapter 30!
YOU'VE TRIED THE REST, NOW TRY THE BEST

¥ø¨æ√´ †®^´∂ †¨ ®´ß†, ~øΣ †®¥ †¨ ʃ´ß†

Michael K. sprinkled oregano, garlic, and red pepper flakes on his slice.

Bob sprinkled oregano, garlic, and red pepper flakes on his slice.

Jennifer sprinkled oregano, pencil bits, and napkin pieces on her slice.

Under the table Michael K. dialed the AAA hotline. He felt a little bad about turning in the Spaceheadz. But he couldn't spend his whole fifth-grade year trying to fix other people's problems, could he?

And he had bought them their slices.

Bob hopped his My Little Pony on top of the napkin dispenser.

Fluffy nibbled the edge of a crust. "Eee ee eeeeeeeeeeee."

"That's right," said Bob. "**IT'S NOT DIGIORNOS**. It's Di SPHDZ. This is very good, Michael K. We knew you would have a good plan. Now, what is next?"

Michael K. listened to his phone saying, ". . . near your alien, then press the star key so that an agent may locate you."

Michael K. put the phone on the table and pressed the star key.

"Ah," said Jennifer. "A primitive voice sound unit. We will tune mind waves to **SPHDZ** frequency! Takedown!"

"Your AI-2100 has been received," said Michael K.'s phone. "Thank you for using—"

Michael K. closed his phone and jammed it back into his pocket. His Spaceheadz problem was taken care of.

"Uh, yeah," said Michael K. "Something like that."

Bob smiled. "We are **THE CHEESIEST**."

A Charmin delivery truck whooshed along the BQE. Twenty-three feet away, Agent Umber reached deep into his refrigerator/closet of disguises.

All systems go.

This was it. The Big One. And Umber had his plan.

Umber strapped on his anti-alien spray, rubbed on his APF 45 alienblock, and pulled up his anti-alien socks.

You could never be too careful.

He remembered what happened to Agent Turquoise in the Montauk Project.

The Picklephone® rang the AAA Top Level code one ringtone.

The *Mission: Impossible* theme song.

Umber followed his years of AAA agent training. He answered his pickle.

"Total confirmation," said a squeaky voice. "Hotline report of alien contact. B-6.357. Go, go, go."

Agent Umber

jumped into his very best disguise.

Agent Umber reached for his shoes.

Holy salsa!

His shoes. No shoes!

Go, go, go!

Nothing in the closet but Elmo slippers.

Elmo slippers would have to do.

Game on, aliens.

Game on.

pHonED HoME
π˙ø˜´ə ˙øμ´

Jennifer finished her slice, then unfolded her teddy bear keyboard/computer monitor/ George Foreman grill with eggbeater antenna.

Bob pointed to the screen with his pony. "So, we will sign up SPHDZ and count to three point one four million and one with our SPHDZ counter here. We will make our SPHDZ network. Build the SPHDZ colony. SPHDZ cereal. SPHDZ theme song. SPHDZ movie and T-shirts and hats and Underroos . . . one hundred percent Total good, yes?"

"Uh, some of that, yes," said Michael K. He edged out of his seat in the booth. He thought it might be best if he was somewhere else when the AAA came in to take the Spaceheadz down. He didn't want anyone to think he was one of them.

Michael K. slowly stood, thinking up a good excuse for getting outside.

"We are so glad you know the next part of the plan," Bob continued. "Because without Michael K. our SPHDZ mission would be bzzzzrt."

"If you didn't show us Walk/Don't Walk . . . everything would already be lights-out! Bye-bye! TKO!" yelled Jennifer.

The little pizza guy with the mustache and the big pizza guy with the tattoos looked over.

"Shhhh," whispered Michael K. "Keep it down. Don't blow our cover."

Bob and Jennifer and Fluffy nodded.

"What do we keep down?" asked Bob.

"Where is our cover?" asked Jennifer.

"I mean, be quiet so people don't know we . . . I mean, you . . . are Spaceheadz. And what do you mean—everything would be lights-out?"

"Wee ee eeee," said Fluffy.

"Right," said Bob. "We will show you at www .Imsuregladthatdidnthappen.com."

Bob pulled a Fisher-Price farm animal See 'n Say out of his Dora backpack. Bob pointed the arrow to the cow and pulled the lever.

The cow mooed.

The See 'n Say spit out a piece of paper with WALK DON'T WALK printed on it.

Bob handed the paper to Jennifer.

Jennifer typed "www.Imsuregladthatdidnthappen .com" into her Care Bear keyboard. Then she entered the code: **WALK DON'T WALK.**

Michael K. looked. Michael K. read. Michael K. dropped back into his seat. Michael K. could not believe his eyes. It was awful. It was terrible.

Michael K. thought about this for exactly 3.14 seconds. And then everything changed.

"So if I hadn't . . . you wouldn't . . . that would have . . . ?" Michael K. stammered.

"Seventy-five percent faster," said Bob. "With more big yuck."

"Sure glad *that* didn't happen," said Jennifer.

"Oh, no," said Michael K. "Wait right here. Now I really have to do something."

And Michael K. ran out of Sal's Best Pizza.

Michael K. stood outside Sal's Best Pizza.

Now the fate of the world was in his hands.

Michael K. realized he might have made a very large, possibly a whole-planet-size, mistake. He had to do something, quick.

Michael K. pulled out his phone. Maybe there was another option. If the AAA showed up—

"Hold it right there," said a voice that sounded like it would be wearing shiny shoes.

A taco stepped out from behind a white van.

But the taco was not wearing shiny shoes. It was, for some reason, wearing Elmo slippers.

"Um. I didn't order any tacos," said Michael K.

"I am not a taco," said the giant taco.

"You sure look like one," said Michael K.

"Thank you," said the taco. "It's my best disguise. I am really . . ."

The taco held up

"Agent Umber. AAA. I believe you called in an AI-2100. What are we looking at?"

"Yeah," said Michael K. "About that, see—"

"I've seen a lot, kid," said taco Umber. "Got it all figured out. Been chasing AEWs all day. Everywhere I go, I see you. I know what's going on. Nobody fools Agent Umber."

Michael K. slipped his phone back into his pocket. He was caught. He could turn the Spaceheadz in. Or he could become a Spaceheadz himself.

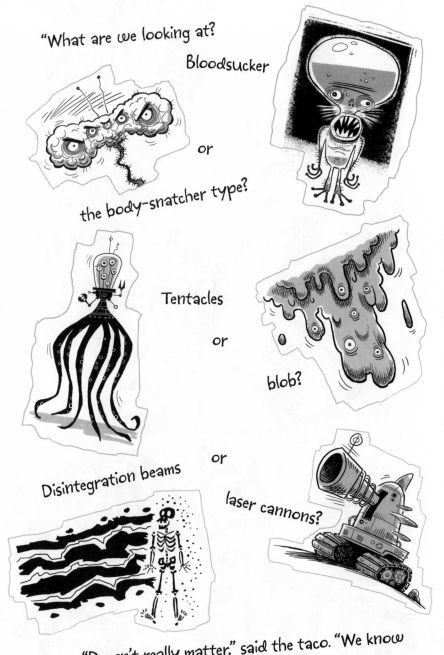

"What are we looking at? Bloodsucker

or

the body-snatcher type?

Tentacles

or

blob?

Disintegration beams

or

laser cannons?

"Doesn't really matter," said the taco. "We know they are terrible monsters. That's why I'm here. They are planning to destroy our world. I take the ... in. We ... the tests. ...

... No ... ... to know ...

"Well, you know ... hat happened ...

... gan again ...

... what happen ...

... cking the ...

... cornere ...

... up in

Michael ...

Michael ... knew ... what he ... and

how he could do ...

... ke it ...

... ate of ... K.'s fifth g ... r,

... ng in the balance of a

YES

Y´ß

...he big moments ...are a... ...ways...
...dramatically lit... ...highlighted y... ...t...
...em are... of... Most o... th... ...ak...
...of the night.

This was one...

Michael K. mad... ...decision.

...K. spoke...

...K. said, "Yes."

The tac... gave a... ...cial...

"Yes," ...tinued ...ael K... ...are right in there."

Mic...e... ...in...te...

"Got it,...

...ache?"

...ael K. nodded. "And the... th... ...

them in. We run the tests. They get disappeared. No one needs to know anything happened."

"Well, you know what happened—," Michael
K. began again.

"Oh, yes, I do know what happened," said
the taco. "You've been tracking these aliens.
You've got them cornered. Now you need a
professional. Again—why I'm here, right?"

The web of a beautiful new plan lit up in
Michael K.'s brain.

Michael K. knew what he had to do and
how he could do it.

"I'll take it from here, kid. What do you
say?"

The fate of Michael K.'s fifth-grade career,
and maybe the world, hung in the balance of a
question from a taco.

"What do you say?"

The big moments in life aren't always well staged or dramatically lit or highlighted by a soundtrack. Most of them are kind of quiet. Most of them sneak up on you like . . . like a soft-slippered taco in the middle of the night.

This was one of those moments.

Michael K. made a huge decision.

Michael K. spoke.

Michael K. said, "Yes."

The taco gave an official nod.

"Yes," continued Michael K. "They are right in there."

Michael K. pointed.

"Got it," said the taco. "The little guy with the mustache?"

Michael K. nodded. "And the big guy with the tattoos."

"The Agency thanks you," said the taco. "Your country thanks you."

"Let me get my friends out of there," said Michael K. "Then it's all yours."

"Oh, yes it is," said taco Umber. "Oh, yes it is."

Michael K. ducked back into Sal's. He got Bob and Jennifer packed up and led them out the door.

Thirty-three seconds later a giant taco charged into Sal's Best Pizza flashing an AAA badge, yelling and screaming.

As Michael K., Bob, Jennifer, and Fluffy walked up the block, they heard noises that sounded like metal pizza pans bonking off a person's head.

By the time they got back to Michael K.'s house, the noises were the sounds of one police siren, two ambulances, three fire trucks, and the chatter of the Channel 11 News Team van.

"Beautiful music," said Bob.

"Wee eee ee eeek," said Fluffy.

"Okay, now I think I've finally got this." Michael K. jumped up from his desk.

Jennifer sat on Michael K.'s bed nibbling a fresh red pencil.

"'Who Is My Neighbor?'" Michael K. read.

"'Number one: You are Spaceheadz. You come from planet Spaceheadz.

"'Number two: On your planet you are waves of energy. Not so much like big-headed, slimy things with eight arms. Everything is waves, so you can change your waves to change what you look like and what you sound like.

"'Number three: You are here because you need to put together three point one four million and one earthlings to be Spaceheadz . . . to make a giant Spaceheadz Brain Wave . . . or else Earth gets turned off.

"'Number four: You have seen my Super-Crunchies commercial and you believe it.

"'Number five: You must not get caught by the AAA.'"

Bob smiled. "*I AM LOVIN' IT.*"

"Wow," said Michael K. "I can never hand this in. We are going to have to just make stuff up about you. Make you seem like regular kids."

"Let's do this!" said Jennifer.

"We will," said Michael K. "And then we have to get millions of people to join us as Spaceheadz too."

"Now we use laser cannons!" said Jennifer, finishing off her red pencil.

"No, no, no," said Michael K. "We need to ask the only ones smart enough to get it."

"Robots?" said Jennifer.

"Kids," said Michael K.

"PRICELESS," said Bob.

"It's all about spreading the word. We'll start with the Spaceheadz website," said Michael K.

Michael K. typed in "www.sphdz.com" to take another look.

"Yikes . . . and we might want to make just a few changes . . . so kids will want to sign up."

"RRRRREADY TO RRRRRUMBLE!"
boomed Jennifer.

"Hooray for Michael K.!" Bob cheered. "He's **GRRRRRRREAT!**"

"No," said Michael K. "If Spaceheadz can save the Earth, Spaceheadz are **GRRRRRRREAT!**"

Fluffy squeaked.

Jennifer burped a whiff of lead and wood.

"And one more thing," said Bob.

"Yes?" said Michael K.

"Now you can tell us, what is toilet paper and why does it make bears happy?"

Superorganisms

They don't win the prize for Largest Organism, but some creatures form into groups made of many organisms. They are superorganisms.

The Great Barrier Reef, off the coast of Australia, is Earth's largest superorganism.

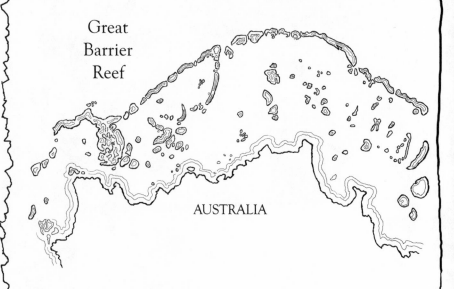

Great
Barrier
Reef

AUSTRALIA

Can you see this superorganism from space?

Oh, yeah.

Chapter 36!

MORE NEWS AT TEN

µø®´ ~´Σß åt t´~

Crazy day in Brooklyn today, Jim."

"No kidding, Kaity. We've got some footage here of the clock on the old Williamsburgh Savings Bank going crazy. . . .

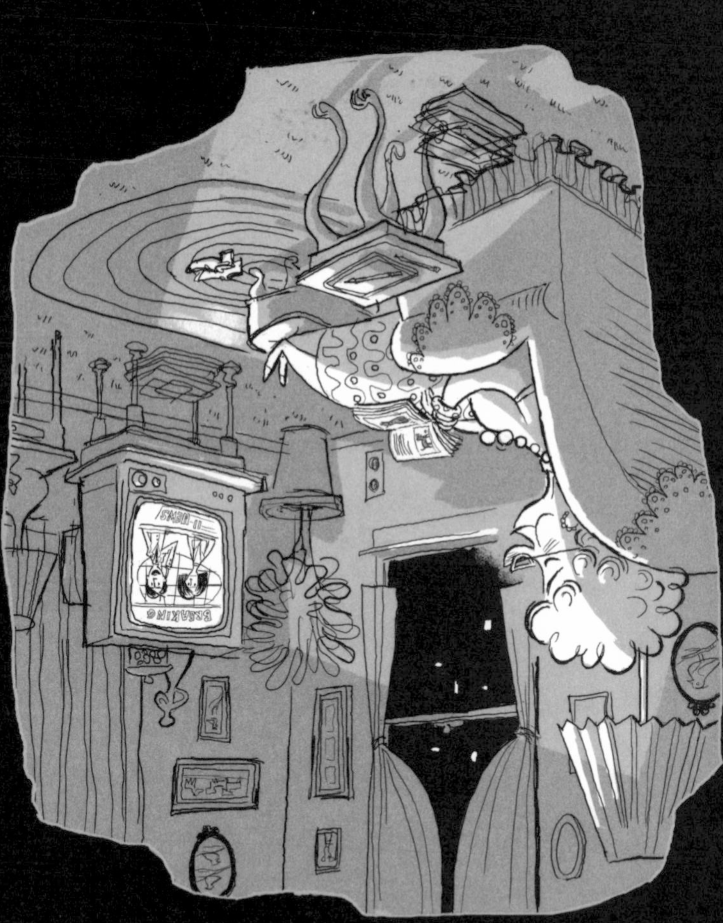

"And then Walk/Don't Walk signs all up and down Fifth Avenue went loopy today . . .

"And finally, a local Key Food gro-cery store sign started flashing this:

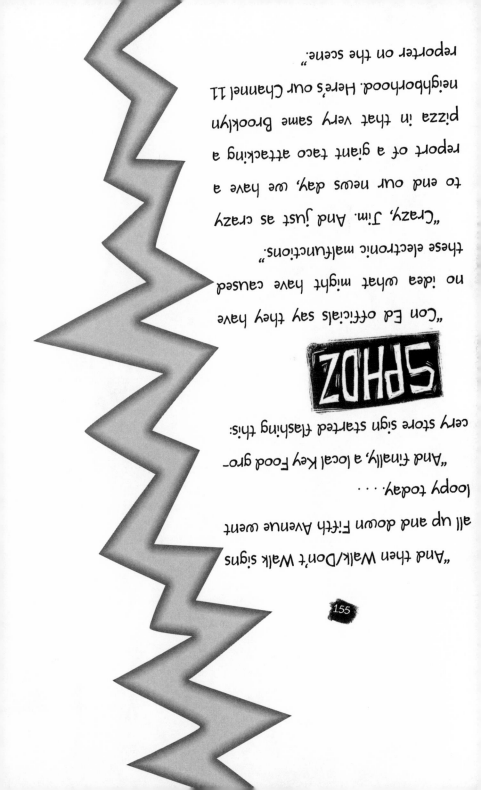

SPHDZ

"Con Ed officials say they have no idea what might have caused these electronic malfunctions."

"Crazy, Jim. And just as crazy to end our news day, we have a report of a giant taco attacking a pizza in that very same Brooklyn neighborhood. Here's our Channel 11 reporter on the scene."

155

HA, HA, HA
·å, ·å, ·å

A broken neon sign buzzed and blinked a watery red light across a small bedroom.

Agent Umber sat on the end of his couch/bed. He rubbed a piece of ice on the collection of bumps on his head. He kicked off his pizza-sauce-stained Elmo slippers.

What had happened? He had the aliens in his sights. They were there. Then, as usual, it all went wrong.

Umber's Picklephone® rang. He knew who it was without looking. It was the chief. And he wasn't calling to congratulate Agent Umber. He was calling to reassign Umber to some new, awful job.

Agent Umber ignored his Picklephone®.

He flopped back on his couch/bed.

The shoeless Umber stared up and studied the pattern of interconnected cracks in the ceiling. He put together his own pattern of interconnected thoughts.

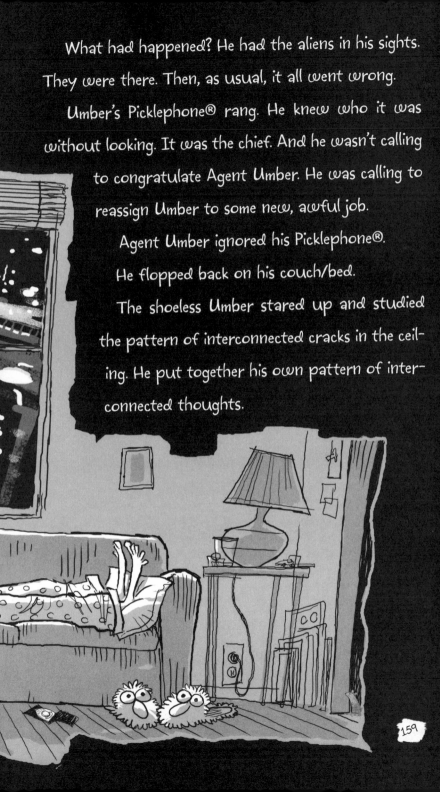

The kid with the skateboard.

Alien energy wave report.

Guys at pizza place not really aliens.

Aha! He had it. Of course—it had all been a big joke.

A prank call. Ha! Ha, ha! Not a big deal. Except for the bumps on his head and the Channel 11 News Team and the chief being steamed and no aliens to show for it . . .

Would Umber let this little setback stop him from Protecting? And Serving? And Always Looking Up?

Umber looked up above the BQE at the stars twinkling over the traffic whooshing by.

No, he would not.

He would work even harder. He would be an even better AAA agent. He would keep looking for those aliens and protecting this world . . . no matter what.

Agent Umber didn't see the UPS truck driving by his window as he drifted off to uneasy dreams of ants and waves and networks. But he might have thought it was a funny coincidence that the big brown truck was loaded with a shipment of skateboard decks.

And the skateboard decks were all Alien Workshop brand.

Building

A termite colony is an amazing piece of work.

So is a wasp nest.

So is a honeycomb.

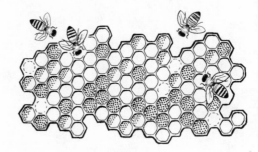

And it's even more amazing that they are all built without a plan, or a boss.

Each termite, wasp, and bee does one small job . . . and those small jobs add up to one big project.

GOOD NIGHT
©øøð ~^©˙†

"**G**ood night, sweetie."

"Good night, Mom," said Michael K.

"Don't stay up too much longer, okay?"

"Okay," said Michael K. "I just have to finish my homework."

"Big project?"

"Big as the whole world," said Michael K.

"Well, the first day of school is always filled with new challenges and new surprises."

"No kidding," said Michael K. as he put the final touches on the Spaceheadz website. "No kidding."

He clicked the **SPHDZ** counter.

The  Name Generator gave him his SPHDZ name.

"Tasty Fresh: Duct Tape," said Michael K. "Perfect. Only three point one four million more to go."